Dinner with the Hummingbirds

Written and Illustrated by
Susan A. Greenberg

McAllister Press
Denver, CO

McAllister Press
191 University Blvd, Suite 254
Denver, CO 80206

Printed in the United States of America.

Publisher's Cataloging-in-Publication Data
Greenberg, Susan A.

Dinner with the hummingbirds / written and illustrated by Susan A. Greenberg. -- Denver, Colorado : McAllister Press LLC, [2014]

pages : illustrations ; cm.

ISBN: 978-0-9907630-1-7 ; 978-0-9907630-2-4 (ebook)
Audience: 3-6 years.
Summary: Amanda watched hummingbirds outside her window from the time she was a baby. When she got older she helped her mother fill the hummingbird feeder and watched them as they fed in the garden. One day when she was 8, her mother forgot to close a window, and a hummingbird flew in and tried to drink from Amanda's juice glass. Although her mother said the bird had to go outside, Amanda wanted to have dinner with the hummingbird, and she figured out a way! Even a young child can solve a problem and have the pleasure and results of hard work.--Publisher.

1. Hummingbirds--Juvenile fiction. 2. Mothers and daughters--Juvenile fiction. 3. Problem solving--Juvenile fiction. 4. [Hummingbirds--Fiction. 5. Mothers and daughters--Fiction. 6. Problem solving--Fiction.] 7. High interest-low vocabulary books. I. Title.

PZ7.G827647 D46 2014   2014916148
[E]   1410

Editor: Pamela Guerrieri-Cangioli
Book Shepherd: Ellen Reid
Cover and Interior Layout: Ghislain Viau

This book is dedicated to Amanda Hillary Cook of Denver, Colorado, and to my young grandchildren, Liam, Freya, and Luna Nash.

A Note from the Author

This book was inspired by Amanda Cook, who was one of those rare souls that surprises you even at a very young age.

I remember living on a lake long ago. Amanda visited there too, on the other side of this lake, once in a while. She was five years old when I met her, just a little blond-haired slip of a thing with a ready smile. As Amanda grew older she would find her way by boat or paddleboat or by swimming with the other children to our wilder side of the lake.

Our shore was sandy and muddy, and the lake weeds would tickle our feet as we landed ashore. We had a large family and Amanda seemed to fit right in with the rest of the brood.

Amanda had a wonderful family that knew ours, and when they wondered where Amanda was, they knew who to call. We loved her.

Amanda was diagnosed with leukemia when she was about nineteen. Her light shown on us until the day she died, and I still dream of her sometimes. A bit of sunshine on a windowsill, a trill of laughter on a floating dock...

Amanda had always loved
hummingbirds.

When she was a tiny baby, her mother
had put a hummingbird feeder outside
of her window.

She could see it from
wherever she was placed.

When she was very little,

she would try
to help her
mother feed the
hummingbirds.

The bright red
nectar was
their dinner.

As Amanda grew older, she would spend many hours watching the hummingbirds in the garden.

They drank nectar from the
feeder and flowers.

One day as she was eating her own dinner,

a hummingbird came in through
an open window. It was hungry.

It hovered over the table. "Look, Mother!
A hummingbird wants to have dinner with me!"

"Amanda, hummingbirds must eat outside in the garden, not in the house."

"Look, Mother! The hummingbird is following me.
It wants my juice! Oh, I so wish it could eat with me.

Could we make that happen?"

"Perhaps.
I have an
idea," said
her mother.

"Let's see if the hummingbirds will
follow the feeder in the wagon.

Then maybe you can have dinner
with the hummingbirds, Amanda."

Amanda practiced leading the
birds around her garden with a
small wagon and a feeder.

Soon they followed her
around her garden.

Amanda's family lived in a
small town called Carpinteria.

There was even a small outdoor café
at the end of Amanda's block.

As Amanda trained the
hummingbirds to follow the feeder,

they would go down the block as far as the café, and back again to her house.

Amanda told the café owner that she would like to have dinner with the hummingbirds.

"Could that happen here?" she asked.

The owner said,
"Yes, they could all
eat outside at a
special table."

Amanda was so happy as she walked to the café with her family, her mom, her dad, and her little brother Alex, and of course...

the hummingbirds.

What a wonder it
was for all to see!

Amanda had
made it happen!
She finally got her
wish. She had...

Dinner with the Hummingbirds!

Susan A. Greenberg lives in Denver, Colorado, and Santa Barbara, California. She has been an artist most of her life and has also kept a journal for almost 20 years. She has always told silly stories at the drop of a hat to the small groups of children that have romped through her life. This book came from one of these fun stories.

Susan has been married to her husband, Arnold, for 34 years. She has a son, Michael, and three grandchildren, who live in Portland, Oregon. She has had many cats, a miniature macaw named Pickles, and an African Grey named Boo. There has also been a large flock of canaries that always find some way to slip into the house. They have entertained the cats a great deal.

She had a shoulder replacement that kept her from painting for about six months. She could, however, when the pain had subsided somewhat, hold a watercolor brush and paint a little every day. And a children's book took shape and color while the author and illustrator healed.

When she is in Santa Barbara, California, a large flock of hummingbirds demand to be fed and will come into her house to find food if a door is left open when they are hungry.

Although the story seems a bit far-fetched, these little hummingbirds will follow the food into your house, if they can. They are clever and fast and perhaps could have followed Amanda down the street. Amanda was a real child that the author loved.

www.SusanAGreenberg.com